Albert's Field Trip

Leslie Tryon

Aladdin Paperbacks
New York   London   Toronto   Sydney   Singapore

Very special thanks to:
BEV BRAUN FOR THE IDEA,
SHELLY LYON FOR THE EXPERIENCE,
NITA GIZDICH FOR THE USE OF HER APPLE FARM,
AND OF COURSE—CON PEDERSON

First Aladdin Paperbacks edition July 2001

Aladdin Paperbacks
An imprint of Simon & Schuster
Children's Publishing Division
1230 Avenue of the Americas
New York, NY 10020

The text for this book was set in 18-point Caslon 540.
The illustrations were rendered in watercolors and colored pencils.
Printed in Hong Kong
10 9 8 7 6 5 4 3

The Library of Congress has cataloged the hardcover edition as follows:
Tryon, Leslie.
Albert's Field Trip / by Leslie Tryon.—1st ed.
p.   cm.
Summary: Albert leads the third-grade class on a memorable field trip to an apple farm,
where they pick apples, watch apples being processed into apple juice, and eat apple pies.
ISBN: 0-689-31821-9 (hc.)
[1. Ducks—Fiction. 2. School field trips—Fiction. 3. Apple industry—Fiction.]
I. Title PZ7.T7865Am 1993 [E]—dc20 92-43686
ISBN: 0-689-84057-8 (Aladdin pbk.)

For the apple of my eye

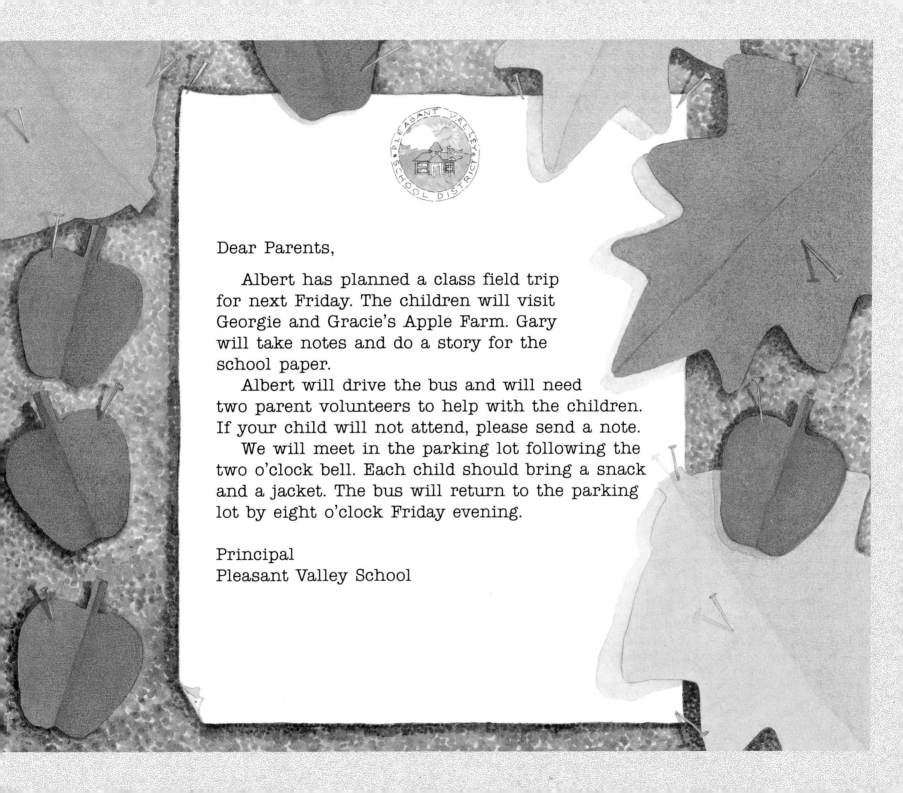

Dear Parents,

   Albert has planned a class field trip
for next Friday. The children will visit
Georgie and Gracie's Apple Farm. Gary
will take notes and do a story for the
school paper.
   Albert will drive the bus and will need
two parent volunteers to help with the children.
If your child will not attend, please send a note.
   We will meet in the parking lot following the
two o'clock bell. Each child should bring a snack
and a jacket. The bus will return to the parking
lot by eight o'clock Friday evening.

Principal
Pleasant Valley School

Ryan got the measles and couldn't go on the field trip. Albert told us that we had to behave and use our bus manners. Albert knew lots of songs to sing on the way. I liked the one about "the thousand-legged worm with the wiggle and the squirm." Albert told us that sometimes worms called codling worms grow inside apples. So we changed the song to "the codling worm with the wiggle and the squirm." It was a long trip to Georgie and Gracie's Apple Farm. Singing on the bus was fun, but that wasn't the best part....

Albert drove over lots of hills. The road wound back and forth
through millions of apple trees. The first thing we saw was a
tractor by the side of the road. Albert followed the tractor down
the road to a big red barn. But that wasn't the best part....

In the barn Gracie introduced us to her sister, Georgie, who runs the farm. We each got our own basket for picking apples. Georgie said we would pick red apples today. "Remember to lift the apple to the sky when you pick it," Georgie said. We could even climb the trees if we wanted to, she said, but that wasn't the best part. . . .

The apple-juice room was cold and sticky, but not as cold as it was in the storage room, where it was thirty-five degrees. We could see boxes of apples stacked way up to the ceiling. We had lots of fun making clouds with our breath, but we were glad to go back out into the apple-juice room.

Bess put our clean apples into the big juicer. It ground up our apples, then squashed them into juice that went through a hose, out a spout, and into our cups. We drank juice made from the apples we picked, but that wasn't the best part. . . .

Aiko made apple pies for us. We each got our own little pie.
Adam dropped his pie on the ground. After we ate our pies,
Georgie gave us a baby apple tree called a sapling to plant in the
schoolyard. We filled our baskets again with different kinds of
apples and got on the bus. We didn't sing about the codling
worm this time. Joy's mother and Willie's dad said they had lots
of fun, even if they didn't know the words to the songs and they
couldn't climb the trees. We all laughed because Albert had
eaten two of the little pies. But that wasn't the best part. . . .

When we got back to the school, it was very dark. All of our parents were there. We weren't really sleepy, but they thought we were. They took us back to our cars, drove us safely home, tucked us in our beds, and kissed us good night, and *that* was the best part.

Dear Georgie and Gracie,

We like your farm very much.

We liked picking the apples. We

liked making juice. Thank you

for the tree. We will be excited

to see it grow. We love you.

Joy

Pat

Jo

Willie

Gary

Mair

Adam

Kathy

Jim